A Small Fire

by Adam Bock

A Samuel French Acting Edition

New York Hollywood London Toronto

SAMUELFRENCH.COM

Cover Design by Bradford Louryk

ISBN 978-0-573-70003-3 Printed in U.S.A. #28044

MUSIC USE NOTE

IMPORTANT BILLING AND CREDIT REQUIREMENTS

All producers of *A SMALL FIRE* *must* give credit to the Author of the Play in all programs distributed in connection with performances of the Play, and in all instances in which the title of the Play appears for the purposes of advertising, publicizing or otherwise exploiting the Play and/or a production. The name of the Author *must* appear on a separate line on which no other name appears, immediately following the title and *must* appear in size of type not less than fifty percent of the size of the title type.

In addition the following credit *must* be given in all programs and publicity information distributed in association with this piece:

**Playwrights Horizons, Inc., New York City,
produced the World Premiere of
A SMALL FIRE Off-Broadway in 2011**

"A SMALL FIRE" was developed at New Dramatists as a part of the PlayTime developmental studio, and also in part, with the assistance of the Sundance Institute Theatre Program

In addition, LORT licensees shall be required to print the biography of Playwrights Horizons, Inc. in the biography section of all theatre programs:

Playwrights Horizons is a writer's theater dedicated to the support and development of contemporary American playwrights, composers and lyricists and to the production of their new work. Under the leadership of artistic director Tim Sanford and managing director Leslie Marcus, the theater company continues to encourage the new work of veteran writers while nurturing an emerging generation of theater artists. In its 40 years, Playwrights Horizons has presented the work of more than 375 writers and has received numerous awards and honors. Playwrights Horizons was founded in 1971 by Robert Moss, before moving to 42nd Street where it has been instrumental in the revitalization of Theatre Row. Playwrights' auxiliary programs include the Playwrights Horizons Theater School, which is affiliated with NYU's Tisch School of the Arts, and Ticket Central, a central box office that supports the Off-Broadway performing arts community.

A SMALL FIRE was first produced by the Playwrights Horizons in New York City on January 6, 2011. The performance was directed by Trip Cullman, with sets by Loy Arcenas, costumes by Ilona Somogyi, lighting by David Weiner, and original music and sound design by Robert Kaplowitz. The Production Stage Manager was Lori Ann Zepp. The cast was as follows:

EMILY . . . . Michelle Pawk
JOHN . . . . Reed Birney
JENNY . . . . Celia Keenan-Bolger
BILLY . . . . Victor Williams

CHARACTERS

EMILY BRIDGES - 58.

JOHN BRIDGES - 60. Her husband.

JENNY BRIDGES - 30. Their daughter.

BILLY FONTAINE - 41. A construction manager in **EMILY**'s construction firm.

One.

(At a construction site. Loud. The door to a trailer. **EMILY** *is wearing a hardhat and is carrying her Blackberry. She looks up at an unfinished building. She yells to an offstage Harrison.)*

EMILY. HARRISON! Get Billy! Get Billy! Get him! Down here!

(She texts.

BILLY *enters. He yells back to an offstage Harrison.)*

BILLY. Because I told him to, Harrison! Tell him! Just! And tell him next time I don't want to hear it!
Bridges!

EMILY. *(Big noise.)* Let's go and!

(They go into the trailer. Quieter.)

EMILY. What was that?

BILLY. Reynolds.

EMILY. Reynolds again?

BILLY. Yeah.

EMILY. Whaddy do?

BILLY. He listens to that fat douche-bag Mitch Hunter on the radio everyday and then he comes in and he spouts off as if he's thought up all that crap on his own.

EMILY. Uh huh?

BILLY. So he's working with Rafi and Jamil and Jeffy and they're sick of it and they don't want to work with him anymore. So I told Harrison "I'll talk to him." and I do I'm like "Reynolds, you know all these guys are from somewhere else right? So when you're saying all this stuff about people coming over here and taking our jobs and, you know you're talking about them." But he's "I've got a right to my opinion!" So I'm "Not on this job you don't."

You shoulda heard Jeffy. He's fucking funny. Jeffy. He's like *(Jeffy imitating Reynolds:)* "I've got a right to my opinion!"

EMILY. I'll talk to Reynolds.

BILLY. Ok.

EMILY. Think that would help?

BILLY. Sure.

EMILY. Ok.

So why's that lift installation down at the Franklin Street job so far behind?

BILLY. It's because of that late delivery last Thursday.

EMILY. Did you call them?

BILLY. Yeah. I called Fat Ollie

He kept going, "It's not my fault! It's not my fault! Billy I don't know why you're pushing at me!" And I was "Whatdya mean it's not your fault? Who's fault would it be?" And then he gave me this long crazy story about this Taiwanese secretary who took the order number down wrong.

EMILY. Whadyou say?

BILLY. I hung up on him and called Randall Bartlett instead and he said they'd make it up to us.

EMILY. Do I need to call Randall?

BILLY. No I got it.

EMILY. Sure?

BILLY. Yeah.

EMILY. Ok. Other than that, the rest of that job going ok?

BILLY. Yeah. McGrath's got too much on his plate though. You heard the story right? about his nephew? and so he's kinda hopeless. I'm working it out.

EMILY. You gonna let him go?

BILLY. No. But I'm thinking about cutting him loose a couple of days and then I'll see how he's doing and suss it out from there.

EMILY. There are a lotta guys who need jobs Billy. It wouldn't be hard to replace him.

BILLY. Come on.

EMILY. I'm just saying.

BILLY. Bridges he's been on four jobs with us.

EMILY. It's your call.

BILLY. And the guys would be

EMILY. Ok. Ok. Ok.

*(***EMILY** *stops. She looks around. Something is different. She doesn't know what it is.*

She gets ready to leave.)

EMILY. Ok. Anything else give me a call.

BILLY. There is this one other thing.

EMILY. What?

BILLY. I couldn't get them down on the carpeting.

EMILY. How much they want?

BILLY. Thirty-nine.

EMILY. What?

BILLY. I know.

EMILY. That's bullshit.

BILLY. Yeah I thought. But

EMILY. Did you sign off on that?

BILLY. I thought I

EMILY. Billy. No. I took you through this before and this is exactly what I said I didn't wanna have happen.

BILLY. I know.

EMILY. Well you don't know. Clearly. Because that's bullshit. And you know I fucking expect better from you.

BILLY. Yeah I know. I just

EMILY. Don't give me an excuse. You sound like Fat Ollie. Thirty-nine? Fuck.

(Quiet.)

You get your invitation to the wedding?

BILLY. Yeah. I sent that little card thing back.

EMILY. Good.

(Quiet.)

BILLY. I think

*(**EMILY**'s Blackberry buzzes.)*

EMILY. Just

*(It is **JOHN**.)*

Hey John.

(He wants to know if they should take a cat that the neighbor has found in her backyard. It looks a bit ragged but cute and it needs a home.)

No. John.

(He thinks it might be nice to have something around the house. It's grey with two white paws. It's cute.)

No.

(Is she sure? It's cute. Ok no. Ok no. Ok he'll tell the neighbor no.)

We don't want a cat.

(Ok.)

Ok. Bye.

(She hangs up.)

John wants a cat.

A couple of months ago every time he called me it was about "disaster preparedness." He went out and bought flashlights and batteries and this radio that you crank this little handle and a whole second set of tools that he labeled "disaster preparedness" and cans of beans and tomatoes and peas and bags of rice and he put this whole kit and kaboodle in the pantry in the basement. With a big wad of cash. So if you're ever broke and hungry, feel free to break into my basement. You'll be set.

No one is going to bomb Connecticut.

BILLY. I do not like cats.

EMILY. What? Cause of your pigeons?

BILLY. Yeah.

EMILY. I can't believe you breed pigeons. I see'm in the park and I

BILLY. No! Come on! Those things aren't pigeons, they're scrapple. I race homing pigeons. They're real birds. They're athletes. I'm gonna take you to a race sometime.

EMILY. How far do they race?

BILLY. Three hundred miles sometimes.

EMILY. Shut up.

BILLY. Naw it's true.

EMILY. Shut the fuck up.

BILLY. I got a new one, Mr. Buddha, he's amazing. You should see this fucking bird fly. He's gonna be a champion I know it. I'll take you sometime.

EMILY. Ok.

BILLY. Some Saturday.

EMILY. Ok.

BILLY. Don't get a cat. Those fucking things are murder machines.

EMILY. We're not getting a cat.

BILLY. That little card thing looked expensive.

EMILY. It was.

BILLY. You're dropping a lot on the wedding huh?

EMILY. Jenny wanted duck and sea bass. With red pepper coulis. I wanted prime rib.

BILLY. You getting it?

EMILY. No.

BILLY. Well. It is her wedding.

EMILY. Yup. Yup.

Ok. Gimme a call tomorrow. We'll work that carpeting bullshit out.

(Exits.)

Two.

*(***EMILY*** and ***JOHN*** in their living-room after dinner.)*

EMILY. Just

(Answers her Blackberry.)

What?

Uh huh.

Uh huh.

Harrison tell him I'm gonna run him over with my car if I have to come back down there.

No no Get him on the phone.

(Holds up a finger "Just a sec" to **JOHN.***)*

Billy put two guys on it. Just put Just put two

Send Pearson.

Send Pearson.

Ok. And put Dempster.

Ok.

Well you coulda thought of this yourself.

(Laughs.)

You're gonna give Harrison a heart attack Billy. Jesus.

Ok.

Ok.

Yeah.

(Hangs up.)

JOHN. What was that about?

EMILY. Billy took McGrath off the Franklin Street job for a couple of days and then he forgot to put anyone else on it and so Harrison's going crazy all over Billy's ass. McGrath's nephew just got eighteen years for possession and intent to distribute.

JOHN. Eighteen years? The poor kid.

EMILY. Poor kid nothing. He beat up his own mother because she wouldn't give him the keys to her car. That's how they found the stuff. They found her and then they got him in her car and the drugs were in the trunk.

McGrath said he knew something like this was coming sooner or later. He said looked at the kid in the crib and told his sister to take him back.

JOHN. He said that to her?

EMILY. McGrath's not afraid to tell the truth.

JOHN. He said that about her baby?

EMILY. The kid's been on drugs since he was fourteen. He hit her with a bat.

JOHN. Get outa here.

EMILY. The kid's a piece of shit. But McGrath's dad is devastated about the whole thing so McGrath's not coming in for a couple of days so he can sit around with his dad and make sure he's ok. He's 78. So.

JOHN. Jesus.

*(**EMILY**'s Blackberry buzzes. She reads a text.)*

EMILY. I need two of me. Sometimes it feels like if I don't do it, it won't get done. Billy's funny though. It's funny watching him He can get Harrison so worked up. Makes me laugh.

JOHN. What are we giving Jenny and Henry as their wedding present?

EMILY. Nothing.

JOHN. Do you want to just give them a check or a check and something for the house?

EMILY. Isn't it enough we're paying for the wedding? I don't want to give them anything else. I don't want her to marry him.

JOHN. Emily.

EMILY. I don't John.

JOHN. They're going to get married. So. We've got to be happy for them.

EMILY. Why? No. No. Why do I have to be happy for them? Who says?

JOHN. They're in love, Emily.

EMILY. He's. I don't have to be happy about my daughter marrying a man who imports cheese.

JOHN. From France.

EMILY. From France.

JOHN. And Italy and England.

EMILY. Cheese.

JOHN. She loves him.

EMILY. He has a speed boat! On a lake! He wears a necklace with a diamond on it! You shouldn't be happy about it.

JOHN. She loves him.

EMILY. We've spoiled her and she's foolish. She's always been foolish.

JOHN. She's allowed to be. She's in love. You were foolish when you married me.

EMILY. Give me another splash of that.

JOHN. What's that?

EMILY. What?

JOHN. Smoke. I smell smoke.

EMILY. I can't smell anything.

JOHN. Emily did you

(Runs offstage.)

EMILY. I can't smell anything.

(Follows **JOHN** *offstage.)*

JOHN. You left the burner on.

EMILY. It's not on. It's off. It's off.

JOHN. Jesus. God damn it. It's God damn it God damn it

EMILY. Just put it Just put it Just throw it in the sink and turn the tap on. John. Just turn on the water.

JOHN. Let

EMILY. Oh give it to me.

JOHN. (*Enters. Followed by* **EMILY**.) Ok That That That. You can't just leave the burner on!

EMILY. It wasn't on, John.

JOHN. It was still hot.

EMILY. It wasn't on.

JOHN. The house could have burned down.

EMILY. Don't exaggerate.

JOHN. It could have!

EMILY. It wasn't even on fire.

JOHN. It was!

EMILY. It was smoldering.

JOHN. It could have burst into flames.

EMILY. Ok.

JOHN. Jesus.

EMILY. It was just a dishcloth.

JOHN. It was a napkin!
You always do this. "It's nothing. It's nothing."

EMILY. Yeah well, it is nothing. Or not much.

JOHN. Huh. Uh huh.

(Silence. They sit.)

EMILY. Why can't you admit it?

JOHN. What.

EMILY. Just admit you don't like him.

JOHN. Who?

EMILY. Henry.

JOHN. I do like him.

EMILY. You do not.

JOHN. That's

EMILY. Just admit it.

JOHN. What would that do?

EMILY. He's not going to be good for her.

JOHN. Who knows who's going to be good for someone?

EMILY. Jenny'll marry him and then after a while she'll really see him for the first time and she'll be disappointed but by the time she realizes she made a mistake she'll be too far in or she'll be pregnant or And she won't be able to get out and

JOHN. Are you talking about them?

EMILY. John.

JOHN. She loves him Emily.

EMILY. I'm going to go do some work.

(Gets up.)

JOHN. Ok.

*(***EMILY*** exits.)*

Three.

*(***JOHN*** and ***JENNY*** in the living-room. They are making the seating chart for the wedding.)*

JOHN. There was a napkin near the stove and it caught fire It was on fire Ok it was smoldering But there was smoke in the room and your Mom

JENNY. Was she drunk?

JOHN. No. No.

JENNY. Sounds like she was.

JOHN. She stood there pretending it was no big deal. But the smell The smell of smoke was everywhere and

JENNY. She was drunk.

JOHN. I think there's something wrong.

JENNY. With Mom?

JOHN. Yes.

JENNY. We know that.

JOHN. Jenny.

JENNY. Nothing a really good therapist couldn't help. But good luck getting her to see one Dad.

JOHN. Jenny.

JENNY. *(A small sound.)*

JOHN. *(Looks at her. Then:)* Don't put Uncle Ray next to Mrs. Dundas.

JENNY. Why not?

JOHN. Because he's left-handed and she's irritable.

JENNY. Where should I put him?

JOHN. Put him between the Smoot sisters. He'll be so excited he won't know which way to look.

JENNY. *(Laughs. Then:)* Aunt Mary'll get mad.

JOHN. Yeah.

But she's gonna get mad at some point anyway so we might as well make him happy.

JENNY. *(Laughs.)*

JOHN. Right?

Steve Carmozzi's coming?

JENNY. Yeah. But Mrs. Carmozzi isn't. I think she's going to divorce him. Mom said.

JOHN. That's a shame.

JENNY. Because of money.

JOHN. He's crazy with his money. He buys lottery tickets by the stack.

JENNY. Yeah if you're gonna win you're gonna win with one ticket.

JOHN. Don't put him near our table. His company owes Mom a lot of money. She didn't really want him to come. She doesn't want to have to say anything.

JENNY. She could have told me that. I wouldn't have invited him.

JOHN. He's an old friend.

JENNY. Still.

JOHN. You gotta do some things.

JENNY. Part of me doesn't want Mom to come to the wedding.

JOHN. Oh c'mon. Don't.

JENNY. I don't like it when she just says things. I know I'm going to be on pins and needles. And I don't want Henry's family to think that I'm

JOHN. Let's get something straight. If you make it hard for your Mom to come to the wedding I'm not coming.

JENNY. I'm already nervous Dad.

(Silence.)

I don't know how you put up with her.

JOHN. She puts up with me too.

JENNY. Oh right Dad.

(Silence.)

JOHN. Put Sam Panday and Juan Pujadas at Alex McCready's table. Alex's daughter What's her name?

JENNY. Molly.

JOHN. She'd get a kick out of Sam and Juan.

JENNY. What about the Williamses?

JOHN. The Williamses. Put'm there.

JENNY. That's a good idea.

(They work on the seating chart.)

JOHN. I'm not the easiest person to live with you know.

JENNY. You are too.

JOHN. No one is.

There was one time When you were at college Your mom got fed up She talked about getting an apartment. She wanted to leave me.

JENNY. You should have left her.

JOHN. I

JENNY. No Dad. You. You. No. You should have gone and gotten your own apartment. Let her live on her own and Let her see how. Because you She.

You might have found out you were better off.

JOHN. Jenny

JENNY. She called me and said these things about Henry.

JOHN. She didn't mean them.

JENNY. She said them though didn't she.

JOHN. She says some stupid things sometimes. She doesn't mean to.

JENNY. They're worse than stupid.

They are.

JOHN. Jenny She's just worried about you.

JENNY. Doesn't feel like worry. Feels like

(Silence.)

And it's not like this is the first time this has happened either.

(Silence.)

JOHN. I did go. I spent three nights at the Courtyard Inn.

I was so

You're gonna I know you're gonna understand this with Henry. Your Mom is tough.

JENNY. Yeah.

JOHN. She is I know she is. But. I don't know how it happens but somehow you can get tied to each other. You're gonna see with Henry. Your Mom and I we're different about some things but I'm lucky she didn't like being alone because I can't. I can't be.

I missed her like

(A small breath pushed out of thin lips.)

Be terrible for me if she left.

Four.

(**JOHN** *sits in the doctor's waiting room.* **JENNY** *enters.)*

JENNY. Where is she?

JOHN. She's in with the doctor. She doesn't want me in there with them. You know how she is.

JENNY. So what's wrong?

JOHN. She's lost her sense of smell.

JENNY. What?

JOHN. She can't smell anything.

JENNY. I ran down here because

(She texts.)

JOHN. What are you doing?

JENNY. I'm texting Henry. He's worried because I thought it was something serious.

JOHN. It is serious.

JENNY. She can't smell anything?

JOHN. No.

JENNY. She can't smell anything at all? Really?

JOHN. It's not funny.

JENNY. Well kinda. Is she like "I can see that big pile of poop over there but I can't smell it"? Because that might be good actually. Sometimes.

JOHN. Jenny.

JENNY. Even if she sniffs really hard?

JOHN. Down at one of the construction sites there was a gas leak and she didn't smell it. And one of her guys was about to light up a cigarette when he did.

JENNY. Oh my god.

JOHN. So it's not funny. It's not.

JENNY. Can she get it back?

JOHN. I was so hard on her when she didn't smell the smoke in the kitchen. Remember?

JENNY. How were you supposed to know?

JOHN. Sometimes it's temporary. From a cold or the flu. But they seem to think that your Mom's

JENNY. Dad. Does she have a tumor?

JOHN. No.

JENNY. Are you just not telling me?

JOHN. No. She doesn't.

JENNY. You promise?

JOHN. Yes.

JENNY. Did they check?

JOHN. Of course. First. They

JENNY. Did you ask another doctor?

JOHN. She's already had a CAT scan and we've checked the house for mold, she's been to acupuncture. Now they're talking about trying a course of steroids so

JENNY. When did you do all this?

JOHN. Your mom didn't want you to worry.

She's going crazy. She's embarrassed. She doesn't know how to mention it to people or if she should. And she is taking so many baths. I don't know why. But she's in the bathroom all the time.

JENNY. She's afraid she might not smell right.

JOHN. Oh. Oh. Of course. Oh.

JENNY. She's gonna be okay Dad.

JOHN. It's weird. Ever since she lost her sense of smell I've been smelling the most amazing things. I was in a Staples Store and the new office supplies Markers and Sharpies and I was smelling gluesticks

And at Rite Aid I opened a can of tennis balls and a mint chapstick and a nail polish and Johnson's baby shampoo and a box of crayons

That thunderstorm last week The rain was And I was outside on the cement sidewalk outside our house and the cement smelled so gorgeous.

And your mom's coat

JOHN. *(cont.)* And the Johnson girl Little Lisa Johnson had a baby and the baby had this toy a little pony A "My Little Pony" pony toy And the plastic smelled so good. It smelled amazing.

*(**EMILY** enters.)*

What'd he say?

EMILY. Let's go. Hi Jenny.

JENNY. What'd he say, Mom?

EMILY. He can't do anything.

(She exits. They follow her.)

Five.

EMILY. Does this shirt smell?

JOHN. It was dry-cleaned.

EMILY. But does it smell?

JOHN. No.

EMILY. That's what I wanted to know.

JOHN. Ok.

EMILY. I just

JOHN. Ok. I'm sorry.

(**EMILY** *purses lips.)*

I had to tell her.

EMILY. It's ok.

JOHN. I did.

EMILY. I said ok.

JOHN. I don't want you to be mad.

EMILY. I told you last week that I didn't care that you told her. Some things could be private but I get that you needed to tell her.

JOHN. Ok.

EMILY. The whole thing is It's nothing.

JOHN. Well it's not nothing. It's worrying.

EMILY. You be worried. I'm not going to.

JOHN. I

EMILY. In the scheme of things it's nothing. McGrath's sister? The one whose son hit her with the bat? Died.

JOHN. Oh no. That's.

EMILY. So that kid. He's in real trouble now. And McGrath is crazy from it And his father And so McGrath is He's worried and he should be. This is nothing.

JOHN. Ok.

EMILY. So this is nothing. I'm not going to let it overwhelm me or ruin my life. I'm not.

JOHN. Ok. Good.

EMILY. Because everywhere there are things that happen. To people everywhere.

*(**JENNY** enters. She has a small cake box.)*

JENNY. Hi Mom. Hi Dad.

EMILY. Hi Jenny.

JOHN. That the cake?

JENNY. It is! It is! It's a sample. They want us to make sure it's exactly right. I'm just gonna

*(**JENNY** exits into the kitchen.)*

EMILY. Don't make a fuss in front of her.

JOHN. I'm not.

EMILY. Don't. I mean it.

(They stand.

***JENNY** enters with a small plate with cake and three forks.)*

JENNY. Try a bite of this.

EMILY. I can't.

JENNY. What? I want you to tell

JOHN. It looks good!

EMILY. I

JOHN. It looks good Jenny!

JENNY. Oh c'mon Mom. Just take a little taste of it.

EMILY. I CAN'T. Not "I won't." I can't.
It's idiotic. But the doctor says
Because I lost my sense of smell, I can't taste things properly. I can taste stuff but it's just bitter or sweet or
That's about as interesting as it gets.

JENNY. I didn't know.

JOHN. This tastes amazing.

EMILY. Fine. Look.

(Takes a bite.)

Happy?

JENNY. No Mom it's ok.

JOHN. I like it. I think it's great.

JENNY. I'm sorry.

EMILY. Nothing to be sorry about.

JENNY. No I am.

I didn't know about the food but I get that your sense of smell is really important. I did some research. It said your sense of smell can influence your mood. That even your memory can be affected because memory's connected to smells so your memory might be So I get it Mom and I'm sorry. I am.

EMILY. You think it's kind of you to say things like that to me?

JENNY. What?

JOHN. Emily.

EMILY. I didn't ask you to find all that out. How do you think that makes me feel?

JOHN. Jenny.

*(**JENNY** exits.)*

JOHN. Why'd you do that?

EMILY. That cake tasted like chalk.

JOHN. What?

EMILY. It had no taste. Neither does this coffee. I can't taste anything.

Six.

EMILY. I can't see anything.

(Blackout.)

John. John. John.

Seven.

(In blackout.)

Eight.

(In blackout.)

EMILY VOICE OVER. This is a horror story. I can feel the devil crouching next to me but I can't see him. He's whispering to this thing inside me that's slowly eating away at me and he's whispering encouragements.

(Lights very slowly come up as **JOHN** *and* **EMILY** *talk.* **EMILY** *is sitting up in bed. She is in a nightgown.* **JOHN** *sits on the edge of the bed.)*

JOHN. Can I get you some breakfast or some lunch?

EMILY. No thanks.

JOHN. Henry dropped by and brought you some bearclaws. You want one?

EMILY. No.

JOHN. You want anything?

EMILY. I'm not hungry.

JOHN. Do you want to get up?

EMILY. No.

JOHN. Ok.

Aunt Mary called. She said, "Tell her I'm worried."

EMILY. Uh huh.

(Silence.)

JOHN. Ok. She also sent a bunch of websites with information on all different kinds of vitamins and minerals and vitamins with minerals and. Do you want me to say anything to her?

EMILY. No.

JOHN. I'll thank her. Or you can thank her tonight at the rehearsal dinner. If you want to.

EMILY. Ok.

JOHN. If you want to.

EMILY. Did she want me to read them?

JOHN. *(Laughs.)* I don't know.

EMILY. Tell her I read them. See what she says.

JOHN. Ok.

EMILY. No. Just tell her thank you. Tell her some of what we've been doing about it all and tell her not to worry. And tell her I'm looking forward to seeing her.

JOHN. Ok.

Jenny thinks we should postpone it.

EMILY. The wedding? No. No. On my account?

JOHN. She just thinks it might be too much for everyone.

EMILY. That's a stupid idea. Don't say that to her. But it is. Everything's ready. Everything's done. So tell her from me "no it's ok." I'll tell her.

JOHN. Ok.

EMILY. People've bought plane tickets.

JOHN. Ok.

EMILY. Let's just get through this wedding.

JOHN. Ok.

EMILY. She's getting married. I'm not stopping her from getting married.

JOHN. Ok.

(Silence.)

EMILY. That was nice of Henry.

JOHN. He said he remembered you saying you liked them. Billy called too.

EMILY. When?

JOHN. You were asleep.

EMILY. Did he say what it was about?

JOHN. No.

EMILY. Can you get me my Blackberry?

JOHN. Sure. Do you remember where I put it?

EMILY. John.

JOHN. There it is I found it.

EMILY. Will you call Billy and hand it to me?

(Silence.)

John.

JOHN. How do I do that again?

EMILY. Really?

JOHN. I'm sorry.

EMILY. Really John?

JOHN. I'm sorry.

EMILY. How many times have you called him for me in the last week?

JOHN. Ok Emily.

EMILY. Turn it on. The button on the top. The button on the top.

JOHN. The one on the left?

EMILY. No the one in the middle.

JOHN. Ok.

EMILY. Is the phone on?

JOHN. Ok.

EMILY. Billy's on speed dial. Just press down and hold the B. Is it dialing?

JOHN. Yup.

EMILY. Hand me the phone.

JOHN. Ok. Sorry.

EMILY. It's ok.

JOHN. I'm

EMILY. *(holds up a finger "Just a sec" to* **JOHN**. *Sits on the side of her bed.)*

Billy. Hi.

Good.

Yeah. Still. No. Nobody knows what's going on. No. It's stupid. I'm

Yeah thanks. Ok.

EMILY. *(cont.)* How are things going down there?

Uh huh.

Pearson did? Fire him.

I am serious. I'm very serious. No. That's not ok.

I don't want to think about it. I want you to do it. Ok?

Tomorrow's Jenny's big day. You're coming right? Can you also drop by today? There's something else I need to talk to you about.

Good. Come by around 2:30.

Ok. See you then.

(Hangs up.)

This fucking nightgown!

JOHN. Sure I can't get you anything?

EMILY. No.

JOHN. Do you want to get up?

EMILY. No.

JOHN. Can I

EMILY. No. I'm gonna sit here for a minute John.

JOHN. It's a beautiful day.

You're going to be ok Emily.

EMILY. I

JOHN. We're going to be ok.

EMILY. I don't know about that.

JOHN. I do. I do.

Nine.

*(*JENNY *helps* EMILY *into her mother-of-the-bride dress.)*

JENNY. Lift your arms.

EMILY. I talked to Billy yesterday. I decided he should run the company for now. I'll be available for advice but I'm gonna start this stuff called orientation and mobility training. So. But in the meantime Billy'll be good.

JENNY. Ok now Just a sec.

EMILY. I gotta figure out how to get around.

JENNY. That sounds good.

EMILY. I'm not just gonna sit here.

And I'm gonna talk to someone about getting a dog.

JENNY. A dog'd be good.

EMILY. I guess it can take a while to get used to each other but I'll get someone to help me. And I guess sometimes there can be a waiting period. But I'm hoping Maybe I'll get lucky.

JENNY. I bet you'll get lucky.

EMILY. Sometimes you gotta just take a deep breath.

JENNY. I'm putting on your earrings. Hold still for a moment.

(Silence while she does.)

EMILY. Which ones did you put on?

JENNY. Your gold ones with the emeralds.

EMILY. Ok.

JENNY. Are those ones ok?

EMILY. How do they look?

JENNY. They look good.

EMILY. Then they're ok. Are you going to put some lipstick on me?

JENNY. Sure.

EMILY. The soft pink.

JENNY. Ok.

(She does.)

EMILY. It'll go with your flowers.

JENNY. *(Smiles.)* It will.

You sure we should have the wedding Mom?

EMILY. Don't be silly.

JENNY. Ok. I'm going to put on your shoes. So I'm going to get you to

Sit down ok here. Ok.

EMILY. Jenny.

JENNY. Sorry.

EMILY. I'm not a sack of potatoes.

JENNY. Sorry. Sorry.

EMILY. No it's ok. I'm

(Silence.)

I'm sorry.

JENNY. How's Dad doing?

EMILY. He's fine.

JENNY. I mean

EMILY. Your father works in HR Jenny. He's fine.

JENNY. Why do you have to be so mean so fast?

EMILY. He's fine Jenny. He has no imagination. You know he doesn't. So he can't imagine what's going to happen. So right now he's fine.

But Jenny. You're going to have to take care of him while he takes care of me. Your father's always been the good one. He's always been the one that people turn to when they're hurt or sad or unhappy. So he's not going to know what to do when he gets sad.

JENNY. I'm going to go get ready.

EMILY. I've got a lot of work to do. So you're going to have to watch him.

How do I look?

JENNY. You look beautiful Mom.

EMILY. Jenny. I think you're very lucky to be marrying Henry. He's a good boy. And he loves you. It's very important to have someone who loves you.

JENNY. Mom

EMILY. And you're a good girl. He's very lucky to be marrying you. You're a good girl.

Ten.

(At the wedding. **EMILY**, *blind. Sits. In silence.* **JOHN** *enters. He is carrying two glasses of champagne.)*

JOHN. Here we go. It's champagne.

EMILY. I don't think I'll have any.

JOHN. Ok. Let's sit down over here.

(He helps **EMILY** *sit.)*

Ok?

EMILY. I am.

JOHN. The kids look so happy.

EMILY. We did a good job.

JOHN. We did. Are you tired?

EMILY. It's hard not knowing who I'm talking to.

JOHN. I bet.

EMILY. Half the time I don't recognize people's voices.

JOHN. You will. It'll

EMILY. They all talk so fast and loud and.

JOHN. You'll

EMILY. And they all act as if I should know who they are. And then they seem hurt if I don't.

*(***BILLY** *enters.)*

BILLY. Hey Bridges! Hey Mr. Bridges.

EMILY. Hi Billy.

JOHN. How's it going?

BILLY. Look at you Bridges! Mother of the bride! You look nice.

EMILY. Don't bust my chops Billy.

BILLY. *(Laughing:)* I'm not! I'm not! I'm not! I'm just not used to seeing you so fancy. You should see me. I look great.

EMILY. You do huh? Does he John?

JOHN. He does.

BILLY. I could be a model.

EMILY. Uh huh. Did Richard come?

BILLY. Yeah. He's sitting over with Jeffy and Jamil. They're taking care of him. This is a great wedding. You guys did an amazing job. Jenny looks really happy.

JOHN. Thanks for your help with the tent yesterday.

BILLY. No problem Mr. Bridges. It was a piece of cake. They were just missing a couple of joiners.

EMILY. How's McGrath doing?

BILL. He's ok.

EMILY. And how's his dad?

BILL. He's ok.

EMILY. Good.

JOHN. Emily, Randall Bartlett is heading this way.

EMILY. Billy can you head him off for me? I don't feel like talking to him right now.

BILLY. Sure thing. Ok. Sure.

(Exits.)

JOHN. He's such a good guy.

EMILY. Is he shitcanned? He's shitcanned isn't he?

JOHN. It's so strange to look out over this wedding. It looks like a high school or It's like a high school reunion. Over near the stone wall there's a crowd of Jenny's lawyer friends They look like the jocks and Bob Ramsey looks like a coach or a guidance counselor and she Miriam Lester she'd be

EMILY. The librarian.

JOHN. Yeah.

EMILY. Does she have those pointy black shoes on that she always wears?

JOHN. And her hair is tied back super tight. Tight for her even.

EMILY. Someone should tell her.

JOHN. And there are all these pretty girls. And everyone is huddled in their groups. It's always the same story.

(**EMILY** *is silent.*)

JOHN. They didn't get that cake. They just got a bunch of plates on this tiered thing with cupcakes on it. It's pretty but it's not a cake.

Henry's uncle Puddy was playing drums in the band.

And Henry's dog They put a giant orange and green ribbon around its collar.

Stanley Williams and Janet are sitting with Tom and Bayla. You should see how bored Bayla looks and Tom looks drunk. His ears are red. Stanley won't stop talking. He's just

Alex McCready is sitting at the table next to them. He told me that his daughter is going to graduate school for architecture and he was saying she'll be building skyscrapers and maybe you could give her her first job when she gets out of school but she was laughing and she told me it's some kind of computer information architecture or something that the kids are building on the Web.

I put Juan Pujadas at Alex's table and I think he's flirting with Alex's daughter

What's her name again?

EMILY. Molly.

JOHN. Right. Molly. Because she keeps tilting her head down and looking up at him like Princess Di and then she

She just did it again She looks up at him and then she laughs.

EMILY. She's a good girl.

JOHN. George just stood up on his chair. That's him yelling.

EMILY. What's he yelling about?

JOHN. He's Something about the strength of a marriage being like a truck and the four wheels of a truck I dunno. Lynn just threw a dinner roll at him. And. Now. Oh. She's trying to pull him down off Oh there

Oh there Oh oh oh oh oh Emily he's down she pulled him down oh he's up he's laughing he's laughing and hugging her and oh oh they're Now they're dancing.

EMILY. He always drinks too much at a wedding.

JOHN. I wish you could see the little Schwartz twins Peter Schwartz's little girls they're cute and they're both dancing with him and with their mom.

EMILY. They're cute?

JOHN. Oh they are.

(He cries. Then.)

They are.

I wish you could see all of this. The light is so beautiful and the tent and the lights in the tent are so beautiful and they did everything in pink and this pinky-orangy and soft green and the light is soft and the light on the cedars that line the lane leading up to the house is beautiful and friendly and everyone looks so bright and warm and our sweet girl

Jenny looks beautiful and everyone is so proud of her and smiling at her and she's smiling and it's something.

EMILY. Where is she?

JOHN. She's dancing with Marcelo.

EMILY. Where's Henry?

JOHN. He's I don't see him No he's talking He's over there talking to his Mom and Dad. What'd you think of them?

EMILY. I liked them.

JOHN. You did?

EMILY. Be too much work not to.

JOHN. You're funny.

EMILY. I am.

JOHN. You are, Emily Bridges. You are a very funny, odd woman.

EMILY. Thank you John Bridges.

JOHN. You always surprise me.

EMILY. I don't know if I want to be here any more John.

JOHN. Don't say that.

EMILY. This is too hard.

JOHN. You're doing great.

EMILY. I didn't love you.

(**JOHN** *shuts his eyes.)*

EMILY. But I love you now. I'm sorry about everything.

JOHN. It's ok.

EMILY. I am. I'm sorry.

JOHN. She's throwing the bouquet. She Ah

EMILY. Who caught it?

JOHN. Stacy.

EMILY. Stacy'll never get married.

JOHN. Now c'mon.

EMILY. You c'mon. Who is going to marry Stacy Gull? No one.

JOHN. Someone will marry her. There's someone for everyone.

EMILY. I dunno.

(**JENNY** *enters.)*

JENNY. Hi Mom.

EMILY. Jenny.

JENNY. How you doing?

EMILY. Good.

(A loud noise offstage.)

JENNY. What was

JOHN. Who

(They rush to see what it is. **EMILY** *sits, staring out blindly.* **JOHN** *returns.)*

JOHN. Emily? Sorry I That was just the I didn't mean to Emily?

(She can't hear him. She sits.

He sits next to her.

Sorrow.

He takes her hand; she is startled.)

EMILY. *(Very quietly:)* Johnnie. Johnnie. I can't hear anything. I can't hear anything.

JOHN. Oh Em

(She takes his hand. Presses it against her face. kisses it.

He kisses her face, her hands. She looks upwards.

Suddenly **JOHN** *can hear everything - a passing car, the flapping of a flag, birds, water, the hum of the world.*

And everything on stage looks very clear.

JOHN*'s eyes open wide as he listens.* **EMILY***'s eyes close as the lights find her, close in on her, and go out.)*

Eleven.

(**JOHN** *helps* **EMILY** *change out of her mother-of-the-bride dress. He mutters now and then as he does it.)*

Twelve.

(**JOHN** *and* **JENNY** *are looking over bank statements and other paperwork.* **EMILY** *sits near them.)*

JENNY. So I got the cable bill and your phone and the internet and the electric and the water bills. Do you have an envelope for your mortgage payment?

JOHN. No. We don't have a payment.

JENNY. You don't?

JOHN. We finished paying off the house two years ago.

JENNY. You did?

JOHN. We had lobster that night.

JENNY. That must've felt good.

JOHN. It did.

JENNY. You paid off this whole house.

JOHN. Yup.

JENNY. That's amazing.

Does the company pay for Mom's phone?

JOHN. Yup. And her car and the insurance. And our health insurance.

JENNY. They gonna let you keep her car?

JOHN. Of course. She'll need it when she gets better.

JENNY. Dad.

Ok.

Is the company going to keep paying for it?

JOHN. Don't you think they would? It's her company.

JENNY. I don't know.

JOHN. At least for a while?

JENNY. You're probably going to have to talk to the lawyers.

JOHN. I'm not going to worry about it right now.

JENNY. Cause I don't know, tax-wise.

JOHN. Ok. I'm not going to

JENNY. Ok.

JOHN. Because.

JENNY. Ok.

What are all those papers?

JOHN. They're from our accounts with Kevin. The stocks and our retirement stuff and

JENNY. Mom ever show you any of this?

JOHN. No.

JENNY. Huh. Maybe you could make an appointment to talk to him.

JOHN. That's a good idea.

JENNY. I could go with you.

JOHN. That's all right.

JENNY. I wouldn't mind.

JOHN. That'd be good.

JENNY. I wouldn't.

JOHN. Maybe it can wait, too.

JENNY. Ok.

Well good thing is, looks like you have plenty of money.

JOHN. Mom set us up pretty well.

JENNY. Your boss said anything about you not coming in?

JOHN. I talked to him a couple of days ago. He said "Just take it easy." Monica is picking up most of my work and her niece is going in and giving her a hand. I've still got four weeks of sick days I've collected so

JENNY. Four weeks! How long's it been since you'd taken a sick day?

JOHN. I don't get sick.

JENNY. When are you going back to work? Are you going back to work?

JOHN. I'm not sure. When.

JENNY. Ok.

JOHN. Because.

(Silence.)

JENNY. So Dad. I want you to hire a cook. Or a housekeeper. You need some help.

JOHN. I'm not hiring a cook Jenny.

JENNY. Dad.

JOHN. You know your Mom doesn't like strangers in the house.

JENNY. She wouldn't mind.

JOHN. She'd mind.

JENNY. I don't like you doing all this work.

JOHN. No.

JENNY. She wouldn't want you doing this much. And you gotta get out of the house a bit.

JOHN. No.

JENNY. She's not going to know Dad.

JOHN. She'll know.

JENNY. How would she know?

JOHN. She'd feel it.

*(**EMILY**'s Blackberry buzzes.)*

JENNY. Don't answer it.

JOHN. It's Billy.

JENNY. Just

JOHN. Hi Billy.

I know. I'm not answering the phone. Too many people are calling.

*(**BILLY** asks if he can come and visit?)*

I going to ask you to

I think we're gonna keep waiting a while on the visits. She's overwhelmed and she's tired. I'm trying to get her to rest as much as she can.

How's McGrath?

*(**BILLY** tells **JOHN** that McGrath's dad has died.)*

Aw. Aw, really? Emily'll be really sad to hear that. Will you do me a favor please Billy, and send some flowers to McGrath and his family from us? I'd

*(Of course **BILLY** will.)*

Thanks. That'd be great.

And say hi to the guys for her. I know she misses you and them.

Ok. Ok. Ok.

(Hangs up.)

McGrath's dad died.

JENNY. Oh no.

JOHN. He was pretty old. I'm not going to go to the funeral.

JENNY. Ok.

JOHN. I'm not going to go.

EMILY. This is so stupid! It's the stupidest of stupid any stupid anything! God damn it! Fuck!

*(***JOHN*** and ***JENNY*** laugh. ***JOHN*** gets up and takes ***EMILY***'s hand.)*

EMILY. John. Sorry.

JENNY. What the hell!

JOHN. She was on a roll.

JENNY. *(Laughs.*

Tries not to cry.

Cries.

Then:)

I'm a bad daughter.

JOHN. No you're not. No you're not. No you're not.

JENNY. I'm not comfortable around her.

JOHN. Yes you are.

JENNY. Henry doesn't want to see her. Because she said all those mean things about him.

JOHN. That's ok. That's ok.

Thirteen.

(**JOHN, JENNY** *and* **EMILY** *in their living-room.* **BILLY** *enters, carrying his hard hat and a casserole.)*

BILLY. I've come over to mow the lawn.

JOHN. Billy. That isn't

BILLY. It's no problem Mr. Bridges. I'm happy to do it.

JOHN. You gotta start calling me John, Billy.

BILLY. This is a casserole that Richard made for you guys. It's got tuna fish and stuff.

JENNY. Thank you. I'll

JOHN. That's

(**JENNY** *takes the casserole into the kitchen.)*

BILLY. She looks pretty good. How are you doing?

JOHN. I'm fine. I'm fine. I'm fine.

BILLY. You think

(**BILLY** *hands* **EMILY** *his hardhat.)*

EMILY. Billy? Is that you? Is that you?

JOHN. Squeeze her hand once.

BILLY. What?

JOHN. Take her hand and give it a quick squeeze. That means yes. She'll know she's right. That it's you.

(**BILLY** *squeezes* **EMILY'***s hand once.)*

EMILY. About time you came by and said hi. I was thinking "Oh he thinks he's too fancy to come and visit me, now he's running the company."

(**BILLY** *whacks her on the shoulder.)*

EMILY. *(Laughs.)* How are you? You good?

BILLY. One squeeze is yes?

(**BILLY** *squeezes once.)*

JOHN. Yeah. Two squeezes means no.

BILLY. I figured the hard hat might

JOHN. The hard hat was a good idea.

EMILY. *(Interrupting:)* John show you that?

*(**BILLY** squeezes yes.)*

EMILY. It's good we figured out this hand thing, huh. Except I have to think up all the questions. But I guess I guess it's ok it's ok because I get to do all the talking. Right?

*(**BILLY** laughs. Squeezes yes.)*

EMILY. *(Laughs.)* As you can see, I'm doing pretty good.

*(**BILLY** squeezes yes.)*

EMILY. How's the gang? Good?

*(**BILLY** squeezes yes.)*

EMILY. McGrath doing ok?

JOHN. I didn't tell her. I didn't tell her.

*(**BILLY** squeezes once.)*

EMILY. And is his Dad doing ok?

*(**BILLY** squeezes once.)*

EMILY. Oh good. I've been worried about him.

Actually John, Jenny? John will you give me a couple of moments alone with Billy?

JOHN *(Squeezes yes.)*

Billy, just give a call if you need anything.

BILLY. Sure.

*(**JOHN** exits.)*

EMILY. Are they gone?

*(**BILLY** squeezes yes.)*

EMILY. How is McGrath, really? Is he ok?

*(**BILLY** squeezes no.)*

EMILY. Is it his Dad?

*(**BILLY** squeezes yes.)*

EMILY. Did his Dad die?

(**BILLY** *squeezes yes.)*

EMILY. I thought so. Damn. Tell him I'm sorry.
I can always tell when John's lying. You're a terrible liar too Billy.

(**BILLY** *laughs.*

EMILY *feels it and laughs too.)*

EMILY. They're treating me like I'm a child.

(**JENNY** *stands and listens near the door.* **BILLY** *doesn't see her.)*

EMILY. I sit here like I'm a big baby. Pretty old baby.

(**BILLY** *laughs. Squeezes yes.*

EMILY *feels him laughing. She laughs too.)*

EMILY. Right?
They're trying to protect me from everything. Which is really annoying. Their hearts are in the right place.

(**BILLY** *squeezes yes.)*

EMILY. But I'm tired of them.

(**JENNY** *exits.)*

EMILY. I'm tired of them worrying about me. It makes me worry about them. Will you do something for me?

(**BILLY** *squeezes yes.)*

EMILY. Will you get John out of the house for me? I don't want him sitting around with me every day. I want him to get some fresh air.

(**BILLY** *squeezes yes)*

EMILY. And check up on Jenny? Will you keep an eye on my girl for me?

(**BILLY** *squeezes yes.)*

EMILY. Ok. Ok. John! John!

(**JOHN** *enters. Touches* **EMILY***'s arm.)*

EMILY. John will you, sorry about this Billy, John will you take me to the bathroom please?
You get out of here Billy. Time's up. It was nice to see you.

(**JOHN** *leads* **EMILY** *offstage.)*

Fourteen.

*(**JOHN** and **BILLY** stand on **BILLY**'s apartment building rooftop. Beers. Couple of empties. Lawn chairs. They are searching the sky for **BILLY**'s birds.)*

BILLY. They're gonna come from that direction.
Richard goes to the movies with his cousin Valerie on race days. He thinks I get too worked up.

JOHN. It's exciting.

BILLY. Shit yeah.

JOHN. When are they going to get here?

BILLY. Still not for a bit yet. Soon.
Just a sec.

(Answers his cellphone.)

What up, Abruzzo?

Where? Fuck.

Yeah yeah yeah. Call me if

(Hangs up.)

That was my buddy Leon. Supposedly someone saw something in Queens but no one's definite yet.

JOHN. Where are they flying from?

BILLY. They were released this morning in Tridelphia.

(Eating peanuts.)

I gotta remember not to eat all of these. I get nervous and I start eating. I gotta save some for the birds.

JOHN. Where's Tridelphia?

BILLY. West Virginia.

JOHN. They're flying all the way from West Virginia? How'd they get down there?

BILLY. We dropped'm off at the clubhouse garage last night. Night before a race we always have a big party with food and everybody together and everybody puts down bets on the birds. Then Joey Masterello trucks'm down to whereever and releases them in the morning.

JOHN. Is that your bird?

BILLY. Where?

JOHN. There, way past there, see, there, look at the steeple and then up.

BILLY. Naw. You made my heart jump. That's a seagull.

JOHN. Really?

BILLY. Yeah.

JOHN. Oh.

BILLY. That woulda been awesome. I woulda been stoked. That was just a seagull.

JOHN. Oh.

BILLY. Good eye though. But you'll see. Pigeons look different in the sky. And before we see'm there'll be a lot more calls. People along the way'll start spotting them. There's a while to wait still.

JOHN. What do you think our chances are?

BILLY. I'm hopeful. I'm hopeful. I got a couple of good birds out there this year. Mr. Buddha, he's a beauty. He placed in three races this season. He's a strong little motherfucker.

Just a sec.

(Answers his cell.)

Hey Jordan! It true?

Did Boxer say that or did someone tell you that Boxer said that?

Call Boxer then. Then call me back.

(Hangs up.)

Fuck.

JOHN. What?

BILLY. Boxer's the guy in Queens and supposedly Jordan talked to someone who talked to him and he said that Little Emerald, she's supersonic that little fucking bird, supposedly Little Emerald is back in already but I dunno how that can even be possible cause I haven't gotten any calls from Staten Island.

Still, might be ok because my birds are going farther and that's all factored in, but still, I dunno.

Boxer's this total dick. He's my nemesis. He's been married, twice, both time to women who didn't like him. He's got fucking terrible taste in women.

(Laughs.)

But he knows how to pick a fucking bird.

JOHN. This is exciting.

BILLY. It's nerve-wracking.

JOHN. Jeez yeah.

BILLY. Wanna another beer?

JOHN. Sure.

BILLY. *(Answers cell.)* Talk to me, Stewie.

Fucking A. Cool.

(Hangs up.)

A whole mess of birds just flew past his roof over in Staten Island.

JOHN. Did he see Mr. Buddha?

BILLY. He wouldn'ta known him.

JOHN. This is exciting.

BILLY. I'm gonna get you hooked.

JOHN. Just a sec.

Hey. It's Dad. Where've you been?

Come on, Jenny. I've tried to get you for three days.

I'm at Billy's apartment, on his roof. We're waiting for his birds to fly home. It's a race. He races pigeons. It's exciting. Yeah!

I know!

She's at home with the new home aide. She was the one who made me come.

Are you coming by tonight? I know she'd like

Oh. Next week then?

Ok. Ok. I will.

Bye.

(Hangs up.)

BILLY. How's Jenny doing?

JOHN. Ok.

BILLY. We shoulda brought her out here with us.

JOHN. I can't believe you got me to come. You're kind of a pain in the ass, Billy.

BILLY. Whaddya mean Mr. Bridges?

JOHN. You don't really take no for an answer.

BILLY. Bridges is Your wife is my boss Mr. Bridges.

JOHN. You should call me John, Billy.

BILLY. And she asked me to get you out of the house. When she asks me to do things, I do'm.

(Answers his cell.)

Talk to me Jordan.

(Little Emerald is in.)

That fucker. Ok.

(Hangs up.)

Little Emerald is in. Goddamn Mr. Buddha better be hauling ass.

JOHN. She's leaving me.

BILLY. What?

JOHN. I.

BILLY. You talking about Bridges? She's not leaving you Mr. Bridges.

JOHN. Sure feels like she is.

BILLY. I guess it must feel like that huh.

JOHN. It does. And no one knows what's going on and

BILLY. But she's not leaving you. She's not.

JOHN. I shouldn't be making this your business.

BILLY. No disrespect Mr. Bridges

JOHN. Cause it's none of your business really.

BILLY. John. It kinda is.

JOHN. It's not.

(Silence. A decision.)

BILLY. Your wife is my friend.

You know, you're not the only one who's had something like this *(happen to him).*

JOHN. I know that.

BILLY. I had a partner, Dion, he was my first partner, my first real, he was the only guy I really loved, before Richard.

He was positive when I met him. He was positive but he was healthy. This was fourteen years ago. All around us We had friends I'd visit them in hospice and sleep there, these little twin beds. And Dion was in the choir at our church and he sang at so many services. But me and Dion He was always healthy and I'd knock wood I was so grateful "Look at us, look how lucky we are," I'd think.

But one day, suddenly, he got sick.

It was scary. Because Why's this happening? and What's happening? and What's going to happen next?

I can remember it so vividly. You don't know what to do. I remember walking down the street Wanting to scream at everyone "How are you going on with your lives, don't you know that -"

Or you think "If I just hold my breath, if I'm just quiet enough, Death will walk by and He won't notice us."

Then he died.

On a Monday at 10:27 in the morning. We were watching Rosie O'Donnell and halfway through her show he died. Not that Rosie killed him.

(His cellphone buzzes. He turns it off.)

Your wife was so good to me. The whole time. I'd only been working for her for a couple of years and I was a mess, I was sleepwalking through work. She was so kind to me. She never said anything but sometimes she got the guys to leave me alone and sometimes she got them to make sure I wasn't alone.

Sometimes she'd be, "Come on Billy! Get going!"

She took care of me and I promised myself, if I could ever do anything for her, I was gonna.

So.

You mind if I say one thing?

JOHN. You're going to say it anyway.

BILLY. You gotta keep doing stuff.

JOHN. I'm doing things.

BILLY. No I mean

This can be a disaster or it can be an opportunity. Somehow. You can try to shove everything back to the way it was, to try to approximate it, to almost be how you were before or you can say "Everything's different and maybe I can be different" because it's a chance to change stuff and stuff you might not have been able to change before.

You gotta live a little bigger than you think you can.

Somehow you gotta still see her. Because she's still here. And life is short. FUCK! There he is!

(Mr. Buddha has flown overhead. They catch sight of him and watch as he flies to the coop offstage.)

Yeeup!

(They run offstage after the bird.)

Emily

Fifteen.

(**JENNY** *and* **EMILY** *sit.*

JENNY *stands, looks at her mother.* **EMILY** *is making a hand-washing gesture, and stroking her fingers, and twiddling her thumbs.*

JENNY *hears her father's car and looks out a window.*

We hear **JOHN** *come through the front door and down the hallway.)*

JENNY. Dad. We're in here.

(**JOHN** *enters.)*

JOHN. Hey Jenny. I thought you weren't gonna come over tonight.

JENNY. Dad, before you go and say hi to Mom, can I talk to you?

JOHN. What

JENNY. Can we Before you Talk Just for a second?

JOHN. Does your mother know you're here?

JENNY. Uh huh.

JOHN. Oh.

JENNY. We've been sitting here for fifteen minutes.

JOHN. Oh.

JENNY. She never really wanted to listen to what I had to say anyway. And now.

JOHN. Jennifer.

JENNY. We're going to move down to South Carolina. To Myrtle Beach. Henry's family's down there and his dad has a friend who wants Henry to help him with his importing business and Henry can keep doing his on the Web and Henry misses his mom and his dad.

JOHN. Ok.

JENNY. We decided a couple of days ago.

JOHN. Ok.

JENNY. I'll come up and visit all the time. I'll come and see you.

JOHN. Ok.

JENNY. I can't do this. I get too sad.

JOHN. When are you thinking?

JENNY. Soon. We gotta pack up. I guess it's pretty easy to find apartments down there these days. We might get a house.

JOHN. Your mom is doing really well Jenny.

JENNY. I get sad about you, Dad.

JOHN. Me? Why?

JENNY. I was telling Henry I was saying "I want to tell him to leave but I know he won't. I know he never will. He's just going to stay in that house and"

I can't stand the thought of you in here. Alone. With no one loving you. And

JOHN. Mom loves me. And love isn't what you get from someone. It's what you give them.

JENNY. She has two different colored socks on, Dad.

JOHN. Your mom loves you so much.

JENNY. Dad.

JOHN. She does. And she's always been so proud of you. She was always bragging about you.

JENNY. When Billy comes here, she talks to him.

(Silence.)

JOHN. Jenny.

JENNY. Will you tell her we're going? For me? Please?

JOHN. Mm.

JENNY. Because

*(***JENNY** *looks at* **JOHN**.

JENNY *kisses* **EMILY** *on the cheek.)*

EMILY. Jenny? Are you heading out?

*(***JENNY** *squeezes* **EMILY***'s hand.)*

EMILY. I'm sorry I was so quiet.

*(***JENNY*** touches ***EMILY****'s shoulder.)*

EMILY. Ok well I love you sweetheart.

JENNY. Bye Dad.

*(***JENNY*** exits.*

JOHN *sits next to* **EMILY**. *Touches her.)*

EMILY. John? How long have you been here?

*(***JOHN*** takes his hand away. Looks at the nails on his hands.)*

EMILY. Is everything all right?

*(***JOHN*** doesn't move.)*

EMILY. What? What is it?
What is it John? What's the matter? What's the matter?

(Reaches for his hand, puts it in her lap.)

John?

Sixteen.

*(***EMILY** *stands, alone in their dark bedroom. She is in her nightgown. It is the middle of the night.)*

EMILY VOICE OVER. I'm dreaming. I wake up and all of this all of this has been a dream. I fell asleep and now I'm awake Thank God Thank God and I'm in the donut shop on Belmont Street, the grubby little shop that I go to with Billy and the guys and I grab a bearclaw and a cup of that crappy coffee and this morning the coffee tastes like the early morning in October when the apples are crisp and the air is crisp and there is pumpkin pie with whip cream if you want it and the girl at the counter is wearing a crisp white shirt pressed and clean and white and her teeth are white and her eyes are shining She's just gotten engaged and she shows Billy her engagement ring and it sparkles so much that my ears hurt ting ting ting ting ting and the guys are chattering and we're all outside and Jeffy is smoking and the smell of the smoke is It smells so good and the noise of the street is so comfortable A car honks and another car honks back at it Mad Mad Mad And I laugh and I laugh

It's

I wake up and all of this all of this

EMILY. I can't do this.

EMILY VOICE OVER. All of this all of this

EMILY. I can't do this.

EMILY VOICE OVER. All of this all of this is still *(the same.)*

It's dark.

It's quiet.

I'm cold. I'm cold. I'm

(A long silence. **EMILY** *doesn't think or talk.)*

EMILY. I'm

*(***EMILY** *cries.)*

JOHN. *(Enters. He was in the bathroom. Touches* **EMILY**.*)* What? What?

EMILY. *(Despairing:)* John. John I I can't

JOHN. No.

(Kisses her.)

JOHN. No.

(Kisses her again.

EMILY *reaches for* **JOHN**. *She kisses him.* **EMILY** *undresses* **JOHN**. *As they start to kiss and touch each other, something of how they loved each other, and how they made love to each other, and how they discovered each other when they were first in love so many years ago, returns to them.*

They make love. It is simple. It is good.

After they climax, they are surprised at each other and they laugh.)

EMILY. That was good.

JOHN. Yeah. Yeah. Yeah.

*(***JOHN** *laughs. Leans over and kisses her.)*

EMILY. Do you love me?

(He squeezes her hand once.)

JOHN. *(Softly:)* You're my beautiful girl.

EMILY. Don't leave me.

*(***JOHN** *squeezes her hand twice.)*

JOHN. *(So softly:)* No. I won't. I won't.

EMILY. Johnnie. I felt all of that. I'm still in here. I felt

END OF PLAY

Also by

Adam Bock...

The Drunken City

The Office Plays:

The Receptionist

&

The Thugs

OTHER TITLES AVAILABLE FROM SAMUEL FRENCH

THE DRUNKEN CITY

Adam Bock

Comedy / 3m, 3f

Off on the bar crawl to end all crawls, three twenty-something brides-to-be find their lives going topsy-turvy when one of them begins to question her future after a chance encounter with a recently jilted handsome stranger. *The Drunken City* is a wildly theatrical take on the mystique of marriage and the ever-shifting nature of love and identity in a city that never sleeps

"A playful and hopeful comedy. Like the best episodes of *Sex and the City,* a little heartache always goes well with hilarity. The cast is appealing, adorable, and top-shelf. There's only one response to something as pleasing as *The Drunken City* - another round!"
– *New York Daily News*

"A lot of fun! Adam Bock's scalpel-sharp insight has made him a potent force on today's theater scene. Trip Cullman pitches the performances at just the right level of wooziness. Tart, smart and intoxicating."
– *The New York Sun*

OTHER TITLES AVAILABLE FROM SAMUEL FRENCH

THE RECEPTIONIST

Adam Bock

Comedy / 2m, 2f / Interior

At the start of a typical day in the Northeast Office, Beverly deals effortlessly with ringing phones and her colleague's romantic troubles. But the appearance of a charming rep from the Central Office disrupts the friendly routine. And as the true nature of the company's business becomes apparent, The Receptionist raises disquieting, provocative questions about the consequences of complicity with evil.

Published with *The Thugs* in a collection entitled *The Office Plays.*

"...Mr. Bock's poisoned Post-it note of a play."
– *The New York Times*

"Bock's intense initial focus on the routine goes to the heart of *The Receptionist's* pointed, painfully timely allegory...elliptical, provocative play..."
– *Time Out New York*

OTHER TITLES AVAILABLE FROM SAMUEL FRENCH

THE THUGS

Adam Bock

Dark Comedy / 2m, 6f / Interior

The Obie Award winning dark comedy about work, thunder and the mysterious things that are happening on the 9th floor of a big law firm. When a group of temps try to discover the secrets that lurk in the hidden crevices of their workplace, they realize they would rather believe in gossip and rumors than face dangerous realities.

Published with *The Receptionist* in a collection entitled *The Office Plays.*

"Bock starts you off giggling, but leaves you with a chill."
– *Time Out New York*

"... a delightfully paranoid little nightmare that is both more chillingly realistic and pointedly absurd than anything John Grisham ever dreamed up."
– *The New York Times*